Don't Walk Away

Don't Walk Away

Sheila Whalum

Copyright © 2019 by Sheila Whalum.

Library of Congress Control Number:		2018914428
ISBN:	Hardcover	978-1-9845-7059-8
	Softcover	978-1-9845-7058-1
	eBook	978-1-9845-7057-4

Print information available on the last page.

Rev. date: 12/15/2018

To order additional copies of this book, contact:
Xlibris
1-888-795-4274
www.Xlibris.com
Orders@Xlibris.com
787069

Contents

Acknowledgements of Love

**To the man who still treats me as his
queen (thirty-six years later),**
the one and only Dr. Kenneth T. Whalum Jr.

To my three talented sons,
Kenneth T. Whalum III
Kortland Kirk Whalum
Kameron Timothy Whalum

To my beautiful daughter-in-law,
Crystal Whalum

To my grandchildren,
Kenneth T. Whalum IV and Chandler Christine Whalum

In memory of some amazing and special women,
my mother, Margaret White Lee; my sister, Angela
Ladale Lee Farmer; and Dr. Loretta Bobo Mosley

In honor of my mother-in-law,
Mary Helen Whalum Rogers (Ormer)

To my dad,

Willie Peter Lee (Dr. Mel Seymore)

To my siblings,

Kenneth A. Lee, Wanda Lee-Howell (Myron),

and Margaret Lee Jackson (Charles)

To the beautiful White, Lee, and Whalum families

**To the New Olivet Worship Center
at Woodland Hills family**

(10000 Woodland Hills, Cordova, Tennessee 38018)

**To the married couples of the New Olivet
Worship Center at Woodland Hills,**

C.A.N.A. (Couples Achieving Newness

Again) established 1999

TO APPLE WITH LOVE

THIS BOOK IS dedicated to my beautiful friend Apple. Apple, the most beautiful and kindest woman I have ever met, became my friend just eight years ago. I knew Apple's story because she told it to me every time I would see her. She would often tell me the story of how she had put her career on hold for many years to help her husband in his professional career. However, after he had finished all his schooling and training and as soon as she was now able to relax and enjoy the fruit of her labor and live the good life, as she put it, he left her for another woman.

Apple then moved out of the home and went to live down south with her two dogs (Yorkshire terriers). When I would see her after this life-changing event, she still could not get over the fact that her husband did that to her, especially after being married to him over twenty-five years.

I started seeing Apple on a regular basis to make sure she was doing better after the ordeal, and she would tell me the same story over and over and over again. She was so beautiful in every way but was also so very sad in her spirit. She was very sad that she stopped caring about herself. I saw it in her eyes, in her demeanor, in her chipped nail polish, and in every other subtle way. All that I could do was to try to encourage her to see the beauty in herself. I tried to help her realize that she did the right thing to help her husband, even though he later betrayed her.

After I got busy with life and not seeing Apple on a regular basis for approximately two years, I found out that she had passed away. I was so sad! I knew immediately that she had died from a broken heart.

So I dedicate this book to my friend Apple with love! She was not alone on her journey.

INTRODUCTION

A Cautionary Tale

TONIGHT, THURSDAY, MARCH 10, 2016, I officially started writing my first novel: *Don't Walk Away*. I had been thinking about many, many things that day because my schedule had been so busy, but now I had time to think more clearly. The mail had come, and my husband of thirty-four years (now thirty-six) had brought it to me while I was cooking dinner. (I know it sounds as if I cook every day, but I don't.) With three grown sons (ages thirty-five, thirty-four, and twenty-nine) who travel a lot and live out of state, I no longer cook as often as I did when they lived at home. My husband, Kenneth, and I often go out to dinner or bring dinner home.

However, once I finished cooking dinner and we had finished eating, I looked through the mail. Included in the mail was *Men's Health* magazine delivered to me in my company's name. I don't usually read them, but for some reason, I started to look through the pages. As I did, I clearly felt that I was eavesdropping on a man's conversation with another man. The entire magazine was all about men empowering other men. I knew that we as women had those kinds of magazines, like *Oprah*, *Essence*, *Ebony*, and *Self*, and the list goes on and on, but I did not realize that men had them too! As I continued to eavesdrop by reading page by page, I was intrigued by what I was reading: how men view women; how they felt about their own bodies, their sex appeal, their diets, and their exercise regime; and how they felt living the life of a single or married man.

But what really stopped me in my tracks was an article entitled "Ted's (Painful, Expensive, but Otherwise Perfect) Divorce." The next phrase said, "In two out of three breakups, the woman decides to call it quits" (Source: *Men's Health*, April 2016 edition). So it was for poor Ted, who thought his wife was happy. Bingo! There it was—a part of the story that I would tell in my first novel titled *Don't Walk Away*. My overriding premise is that there are wives who leave their husbands after many years of marriage and husbands who don't even have a clue until it is too late because they never see themselves as they are but the wives do!

In the *Men's Health* article, I read about Ted's wife, Sarah, who leaves the marriage after more than ten years. The five wives you are about to meet leave their husbands after twenty-five plus years. The question is, Why couldn't they stay married after investing so many years of their lives in a marriage they vowed to remain in until death do they part?

CHAPTER 1

Sincerely, Ann

FEBRUARY 12, 1958, was a day that would forever be remembered. It was two days before Love Day, which was considered Valentine's Day. Christmas had passed, winter was slowly leaving, and Valentine's Day was on its way.

He was nice looking, tall, and slim. He had a nice smile with good teeth and always wanted to show them to the world. He worked as a carpenter, fixing up houses around town in Nashville, Tennessee, and it seemed everybody knew him. He always wore those cowboy boots and hats. In his line of work, he constantly saw all kinds of women driving by or walking by.

He even fell off a ladder several times when an attractive lady would walk by and speak.

When Jenny Ann Brussel walked by and spoke, "Hi, how are you?" he was looking at her so hard that he couldn't answer, and he fell in a pile of dirt. She stopped to help him get up and to see if he was okay. She said, "My name is Jenny Ann, but you can call me Ann."

He quickly said, "Well, hello, Ann, my name is Pierre Tyde.

I know it is a strange name around here, but my mother knew someone in her past named Pierre. So she named me Pierre, but guess what? I never met Pierre, and I don't look like the man I call Dad." Pierre continued, "Where did you come from? I have never seen you around here before?"

Ann said, "I live in the neighborhood with my grandmother."

Since Pierre had a contract to do work on this particular house for approximately three months, he got to know Ann quite well. She would pass him every day when she got off the bus. Ann was seventeen years old and was very short, and she thought Pierre was much too tall.

However, she enjoyed him looking her up and down when she would pass by him. Finally, one day, after Pierre kept seeing this fine five-feet-three woman passed by, he got the nerve to ask Ann out on a date. He said, "Ann, how about going to eat on Friday evening when I get off work at six?"

"Sure!" she answered immediately. "That sounds great! I live at 3256 Sand Lawn, which is around the corner in a dark-green house."

Pierre said, "I will see you then."

Pierre had one sister whose name was Paula. His dad tended to spend more time with him, and his mom spent more time with his sister. Therefore, Pierre pretty much got what he wanted out of life. He was eighteen, so he was able to go to many places for adults. He was dating three girls at one time, but when he met Ann, everything changed. He knew he had to have her for more than just a friend and a sidepiece number 4.

After one year of Pierre and Ann dating, when she turned eighteen, he decided it was *time*—time to *pop the question*, that is. He thought there was no need for waiting. They were both in love with each other. He loved how she walked, and she loved how he smiled. So he asked her to marry him. Since she had come to live with her grandmother, who was somewhat strict, she said yes. "Yes, I will marry you, but my cat Bloomingdale has to come too, or it's a deal breaker."

Pierre said, "It is so!"

Image here

Pierre and Ann were in a hurry to get married. After all, they were in love, and love waits on no one. They decided to get married on Valentine's Day, February 14, 1959. Ann wanted a very small intimate wedding.

Ann's pastor, Reverend Morris of True Religion Church, No.2, performed the wedding ceremony at 4:00 p.m. Ann remembered saying, "With this ring, I thee wed," while looking into Pierre's slender face.

The next day she said, "Did I really do this? Did I really get married?"

Pierre said, "Yes, honey, we did!" Ann later learned the true meaning of the phrase "God bless the child that's got his own!"

God Bless the Child That's Got His Own

Pierre and Ann moved into a duplex. Ann was so proud of it. She had become the perfect wife to Pierre.

She started doing everything that she had learned from her grandmother. She kept the house clean, cooked, and made love to him at the drop of a hat when he wanted it. She did everything she thought she was supposed to do. She even made a Monday-to-Sunday calendar as to what they would do on a weekly basis. This great marriage went on for approximately five years, but then Pierre started changing. Ann was not aware of Pierre's history, but she was about to find out. She knew within her heart that something wasn't right between them. He no longer came home on schedule. He started coming home later and later.

Pierre would start his same old tricks again when working as a carpenter, flirting with women, even prostitutes. What he didn't know was that his wife, Ann, had been a stripper in her teenage years. She did not share that information with her husband, however. She was known as Candy-apple, and boy, she could make it "rain." She had learned the tricks of the trade from her mother who had a full-time job at the Destiny Strip Club and would often bring Ann because she couldn't get a babysitter to keep Ann late in the midnight hour, and that caused serious problems for Ann. She was molested several times by different men while waiting on her mother over in the midnight hour.

After months of witnessing Pierre's behavior that reminded her of some of the tricks she used to play as a stripper, Ann decided to take matters in her own hands. She decided to go and see just what her husband was doing and why he wasn't coming home on time. One Thursday evening, she drove to where he was working, and she parked her car in a secluded spot where she could see him clearly. When she saw how Pierre was looking at a known prostitute named Leah, who had just walked by him the same way she had walked by him when they met, and when she saw how he was flirting with such a trashy woman, something rose up in her that she couldn't contain. Then before she knew it, she pulled up alongside him and shouted to Pierre, "I hate you, you bastard!" and drove off.

Ann was slowly seeing more and more signs of Pierre's infidelity—the usual not coming home on time (sometimes five or six hours later), not wanting dinner, and not being interested in lovemaking anymore. She didn't want a divorce; she just wanted her marriage back, like it was in the beginning. She wanted to feel that newness again.

When Pierre made it home, she told him to sit down. Then she and Pierre talked about what she had seen. "It's clear to me that you want the best of both worlds, Pierre, and I'm not having it," said Ann.

"Ann, you're overreacting. It's not that big of a deal. You know I love you," said Pierre. And so, she accepted his opinion and then had her own opinion but didn't tell Pierre.

They did not have children, so she decided that she would get a job. She would go back to being a stripper since he would not stop his bad habits. Because of her molestation as a young girl and because of Pierre's new ways, something in her snapped, and she no longer wanted to be the perfect wife. Ann called her old boss, Sam. "Hello, Sam, remember me?"

"Well, hell yeah!" said Sam. "You were Cinderella! How could anyone forget you with a body like that?"

Ann said, "I know it's been a while, but I need to come back to work."

Sam said, "Cinderella, you don't have to tell me twice. You can start today!"

But as soon as she had made up her mind to get a job at the age of twenty-four, she started feeling very sick. She did not know what was going on with her, so she went to the doctor, and she got the news of her life. Dr. Smith said, "Ann, you are pregnant!"

After receiving the great news that she was going to have a baby, Ann realized she could not do the job as a stripper. She called Sam and said, "Thank you, Sam, for the opportunity, but

Cinderella won't be back. She is pregnant." Pierre never found out about the fact that she had once been a stripper. Ann had their beautiful son and named him Samuel. She stayed at home and cared for their son and her husband full-time. Life went on as usual for several years.

After six years of marriage, Ann found out that Pierre was going to strip clubs in the evenings before going home. She realized that if she had taken that job years earlier, he would have possibly seen lecherous men *making it rain* on his own wife!

Since they now had a child, this situation was not going to work out. Ann told Pierre to stop it. Pierre did stop and started back loving Ann liked he used to when he first laid eyes on her. They started making hot passionate love until she got pregnant again with their second child. Pierre realized he had to work more as a carpenter with another child coming.

Things were going pretty good again, until Red came into the picture. Red started walking in front of Pierre and Ann's house. Red was another prostitute that Pierre knew, but she was too close to home. When Ann realized what was going on, she blew a gasket. She asked Pierre, "You now have your hoes coming in front of our house? I am pregnant with your second child, and you bring this drama to our home?"

The downward spiral to hell had started. Even in the midst, Ann had to take care of their kids, Samuel and Anna Rose, while the drama continued for many years. Ann was no longer happy in the marriage and could not come to grips with Pierre's attraction to such "trash." She said to Pierre, "We have these two beautiful children, so how could you do this to me?" But Pierre was hooked on the hoe. He couldn't and wouldn't leave her alone. Ann decided to accept it because she didn't have a job and she had two children that needed to be taken care of.

Why Are You Hurting Me?

Ann could not figure out why Pierre would hurt her the way that he was. She thought that they would love each other "until death do them part." But it didn't happen that way. Pierre had gotten tired of Ann always accusing him of something, until one day, he snapped and hit her. He started his first round of domestic abuse. He knocked her down on the floor and then put his foot in her chest. "Pierre, what are you doing? I Love You! I did not mean to make you mad or upset. Please don't hurt me!"

I Am Trying to Help You

Pierre shouted back to Ann, "Why do you keep accusing me of messing around with prostitutes and hoes as you call them?"

Ann said, "Because as a wife, I know. Pierre, please let me get up off the floor so that we can talk about it." Pierre let Ann up off the floor, and she said to him, "I am just trying to help you. Pierre, it is as if you are no longer the man I fell in love with. You are no longer the man who always had a smile on his face."

I Am Now a Whole Different Person Than I Was

Ann continued, "Please tell me what is bothering you. I am your wife, and I want to help."

Pierre decided to open up to Ann. "I am now a whole different person than I was. You see, I didn't know my real father, and it must be something in my DNA. I felt that I always had to be in charge of my own life. I just had a feeling. I knew that I was not going to allow a woman to manipulate me in any way, so right after we got married I noticed some changes in you and knew that I was not going to be the kind of man that people called henpecked." Ann accepted Pierre's explanation, and they continued their journey with their marriage for the next ten years.

Why Are You Bullying Me?

After the children had gotten older, they left home. Samuel went off to live with his girlfriend, and Anna Rose went to Kansas City to Missouri Cosmetology School. However, Pierre started up again. Ann noticed that he had gotten worse since the earlier years. She asked Pierre, "Why are you bullying me? Why are you raising your voice at me? I didn't do anything to you." Pierre looked incredulous, but she continued, "I just asked what you wanted for dinner, and you went totally off the wall! You even started shaking and trembling!" Ann knew in her heart that he had been trying to do better and not live in that old way of calling in hoes and prostitutes, but it was almost like he was having a fit: *jonesing* if you will, looking for that next high.

It's Not the End of the World

"Pierre, it is not the end of the world. I am here, and I am here to help you." And Ann did! She did everything humanly possible for her husband that she could, but it was not good enough. She really needed to talk to someone she trusted. She had three friends named Brenda, Taylor, and Edith. She tried to decide who among them she could tell about her situation, but neither of them were able to handle it: Brenda's elevator did not go all the way to the top, and Taylor and Edith had shown jealousy signs to her on many occasions. So she just decided to deal with the situation on her own.

I Am No Use in This Marriage

Ann started thinking, *I am no use in this marriage. No matter what I do, it is not good enough.* One evening, she decided that they would have a very special romantic evening. She went to Trousseau Boutique and bought a red negligee with the front out. She put her hair up in a bun, put on red lipstick, placed rose petals on the bed, and had the music and wine just right.

When Pierre walked in the house, he said, "What is this?"

Ann quickly said, "It is all for you. I want to love you like no one else can. Pierre, you are the man of my dreams. When I first met you, I knew that you would be my husband."

Pierre could not wait to strip me down naked. He started at the door. We immediately got busy! Everything was just right—the mood, the music—and Pierre loved the perfume I was wearing. "What are you wearing? It smells so good."

"Oh, thank you! It is Estee Lauder," stated Ann.

"Well, I will never forget that smell," said Pierre.

We started making hot passionate love until Pierre called me out of my name and called me Spicy. I said, "Who is Spicy? Another one of your hoes' names?" I pushed him off and said, "You got the wrong one. I am Ann, your wife,-remember?"

Pierre said, "Ann, I am so sorry! I was so caught up in the moment. Your perfume got to me. That is what Spicy wears."

"Oh, so you bought Spicy, your hoe, the same kind of perfume as your wife?" said Ann.

Pierre could not deny it when Ann confronted him. "I am so sorry, Ann," said Pierre.

Ann said to Pierre, "I am no use in this marriage. I cannot go on like this! It's killing me!"

Ann decided to take matters in her own hands. Since Pierre had started staying out late again at the strip clubs and she felt that since she was not getting "it" at home, then she would get "it" from someone else. Ann felt that she needed to get back in the game. She wanted more sex too since her husband was getting more sex.

She knew that it was wrong, and she thought of her grandmother, but she had to get back at Pierre for hurting her the way that he did. Since she knew the exact time that Pierre would arrive at home, she would allow different men whom she had met years ago to come by the house for "it." Pierre did not have a clue.

Happiness Is Being Content with Myself

Ann said, "I have got to be content with myself for happiness is being content with myself." She started changing. She knew that if she was going to survive for herself, she had to do something. She took the focus off him and put it back on herself. Somehow, she thought that if she used reverse psychology, things would change. *If he thought I was really happy, then he would treat me better.* Ann started dressing up more, getting her hair done often, getting her nails manicured, and putting on more make-up and more perfume. She started thinking and getting her mind back in order.

What Do People Know Me For?

Ann asked herself, What do people know me for? Do they know me for me, or am I just Pierre's wife to them?

Don't Place Your Life Outside of Yourself (Prince)

Ann came to a realization: "Don't place your life outside of yourself" (Prince). That was what she did. She was no longer the pretty Ann, who would walk by, and men would stop in their tracks. She used to be like those women whom she had read about.

They had it going on, and I did too. And so as usual, that led to me being singled-out. I was a good catch. I, like many of them, got married, but slowly over time, things changed drastically.

He Had Me Running Around in Fear

Pierre had Ann running around in fear—fear of the unknown and fear of destiny. She thought to herself, *Do I want to live like this for the rest of my life? My answer is no! Hell, no!*

Why Don't You Like Me?

One day Ann asked Pierre, "Why don't you like me?"

He said, "I do like you. I even love you. It's just that you don't like yourself." His answer startled her. Somehow, he twisted it to make it as if she was crazy.

He actually acted self-righteous, as if he didn't have a clue about what she was talking about. As she looked at him in his glazed eyes, she thought to herself, *I can either help this man or leave this man.*

Don't Give Up on Yourself

Ann decided to leave Pierre after *twenty-six years* of marriage because a light bulb came on in her head. She remembered something that Mrs. Shelton, her eighth grade science teacher at Viewpoint Middle School, told the class one day. They were all doubting themselves because the class was so hard, and she told all of them, "Don't give up on yourselves!"

Her mind went back to the present, and she told herself, "Don't give up on yourself." With that statement, she didn't. She started loving herself all over again! The feeling was so wonderful! She got freedom! She let go of the fear of the unknown.

Applause Is Like Waves of Love

Ann had heard that "applause is like waves of love." *Bamm! There it was. I was able to do it for myself.* She applauded herself for the lessons she had learned in her marriage to Pierre, and she applauded herself because she had the courage to get up and do something about it.

The Knowledge I Gained Over the Years

The knowledge that Ann had gained over the years—the good and the bad—taught her that the only thing that could matter was herself.

Called the Marriage Repairman

Ann would often tell her grandmother, "I should have left Pierre after ten years of marriage." Then it became twenty years of marriage, and then after twenty-six years of marriage, it clicked. Ann got up that morning and made Pierre's breakfast as usual. He went to work; she cleaned the house and then wrote him a letter:

Dear Pierre:

I have always loved you. I love you even as I write this letter, but I have to leave you for good. I can no longer accept your "private lifestyle" of other women. I can no longer go through this again, time and time again, after the very first time. I wish you well, but I am no longer your number 1 hoe.

Sincerely,

Ann

Ann, then called the marriage repairman by her divorce attorney, and ended the marriage of *twenty-six years*. She left that day and started a new life. She became a certified fitness trainer since she loved to walk and exercise when she was a little girl. She went back to her first love—herself.

CHAPTER 2

Merry Christmas, Baby!

*M*ENTAL BITCH—YES, THAT is me because that is what he *made* me. My name is Prada, and my husband is Truce. Truce and I met at a Christmas party in 1975. He was twenty-six, and I was twenty-three. He is white, and I am black.

My best friend Carolyn asked me to go with her to the annual Christmas party that the Federal Express was having. She had been invited by another friend of hers, so I agreed. We were living in Houston, Texas, located on the Gulf of Mexico, where it didn't get too cold in December, so I was able to wear this fabulous sleeveless dress that was emerald green.

My hair was cut in a cute bob, and I wore emerald earrings that highlighted my face. When I walked inside Hilton, all eyes were on me, and I knew it. And then here comes this fine man coming toward me.

"Hello, my name is Truce Nelson."

"Hi, Truce, my name is Prada Yoke, and this is my friend Carolyn."

"Hi, Carolyn. I haven't seen you beautiful ladies around here."

"Well, apparently, don't hit all the hot spots because we do. We love to party!"

"Well, that's great, and I love to party too though I am a pastor."

"A pastor?" Prada shouted!

"Yes, a pastor! I am still young, but I like to party too!"

"Okay!" shouted Carolyn.

As the Christmas party continued and the evening was getting late, Truce asked for my telephone number and wanted to take me home, but I said, "No, thanks! I will leave with Carolyn, but here is my telephone number."

The very next day, Truce called and wanted to see me. He wanted to take me out to eat at Finland's, a popular burger joint. It was my favorite, so I obliged. We actually met there because we had just met the night before, and I didn't want to take it too fast. Once there and seated, we really got to know each other.

Staying Alive

"So, Prada, tell me about yourself."

"Well, I graduated from Houston High School and then went to the University of Houston and got a degree in political science. I now teach at a local high school. I have two older brothers. One lives in San Diego and the other one in Washington, DC. What's your story, Truce?"

"As, I mentioned to you, I am a pastor. I have been pastoring for four years. I oversee the Mountain Ranger Church in downtown Houston."

"What?" asked Prada. "That's your church? I pass that church all the time."

"Prada, I am recently divorced. I was married for six years, but we started having major issues and couldn't seem to resolve them, so we went our separate ways."

As I was listening to all he was saying, he told me he had no kids. I thought, *Okay. Not bad! I think I can work with this situation.*

Truce and I continued to see each other because we really enjoyed each other's company. He even asked me to go out of town with him to a preacher's conference in Kansas City. I went, and boy, we had the time of our lives. I thought, *This must be heaven. If not, we were mighty close.*

He wined and dined me like I had never experienced before. Nine months later in September, he asked me to marry him. He did not want another big wedding, like he had with his first wife. He just wanted one of his preacher friends to come over to the church and marry us. I asked him, "Truce, why do you want to get married so quickly after a divorce?"

Truce answered, "This is my way of staying alive."

We got married at 6:00 p.m. on Sunday, August 22, 1976, in his office. Mountain Ranger Church did not have night service like a lot of churches I know, so we were able to have a private ceremony. I didn't necessarily need a big wedding because he had proven to me that this marriage was the one for him, and he assured me that this marriage would last for a lifetime. I believed him!

I moved into his beautiful home with all the trimmings. He even bought me a new car to match my new status as first lady of Mountain Ranger Church (even though my Fiat was fine for me).

When I was introduced to the church that following Sunday morning after the marriage ceremony, to my surprise, the members embraced me in a way that I did not expect. They greeted me with cheers, hugged me almost to death, and even gave me gifts that day! I thought again, *Wow! This must be heaven.*

He's My Savior

Truce became my savior. He did everything for me and gave me everything. Then I gave him his first son, Truce Jr. *Lord, have mercy!* As I said many times, this must be heaven.

Five years had passed, and things were really wonderful! I had gotten a promotion on my job! Truce Jr. had started prekindergarten, and the church was doing quite well.

The women were getting ready for a women's conference and asked me to come one Saturday morning. I got there a little early before the rest of the women came. So there were maybe five or six women sitting around and talking. They started talking around me about a woman name Brenda. I just listened because I wanted to hear what they would say and to see if it was different from what Truce had already told me.

A lady named Sela said, "I remember when Brenda first came to the church with a dress so tight I thought she was going to pass out! And do you remember how Deacon Ray got all choked up and almost had a heart attack when she passed by the offering table?"

"Yes, Lord!" said Samantha. "He just couldn't take it!'

What I found out that day was that the church people, especially women, could be messy. As I already knew, Brenda was Truce's girlfriend before he married the first time when they were younger. She had followed him over to the church when he became a pastor and had given his first wife some problems.

I learned that church people would tell you everybody's business if they knew it, and they also knew their pastor's business. I listened long enough until the other women started coming in for the conference. I let the conversation ease out of my head and went on about my business as usual.

Sister Lottie called the conference to order. She said, "Women, welcome to It's All About You Conference, and we are about to have the time of our lives!"

After the conference, I met up with my friend Carolyn at the mall. We were both shopaholics! We usually shopped together once a month. I told her about the women's conference that I had just left at my church and what they were saying about Truce, my husband and the pastor. It was as if I did not know whom they were talking about. And Carolyn said, "Well, I have heard some things too! He had the need to touch all the women he met, but that was before he married you. I do not know if he is still doing that or not *after* he married you."

I started thinking, and I remembered that no matter where we were, if a woman was anywhere around, he felt that he had to make himself known and touch her skin in some way. Though it was never in an inappropriate way, I noticed this side of my husband.

Doctors, Lawyers, and Preachers—Oh My!

When I got back home that evening from the conference, I never said anything to Truce about what the women at the church had said, nor my friend Carolyn because I had heard that doctors, lawyers, and preachers often had many side chicks, but I didn't think too much about the preachers. After hearing the women gossip, I thought, *Oh my! What have I gotten myself into?*

Truce and I continued to love our marriage and continued to be happy until I started noticing a change in him. He was slowly changing into this different man.

My mind started going here and there about his past: maybe he is talking to his old wife again, maybe he is talking to his old girlfriend who is still at the church, or maybe he is talking to someone new.

While shopping again with my friend Carolyn, she would always bring up the point about Truce touching women. Maybe she was trying to tell me something, but I never entertained it. After several shopping trips with Carolyn over several months, I had to finally drop her like a hot potato because she would not drop the "touching" conversation about my husband. And I did not need that kind of friendship.

One Thursday evening, Truce called me, "Hey, baby, I will be home late, so don't worry about dinner. I have to take care of some important business."

I said, "Okay, that's fine." After that conversation, I told Truce Jr. that we were going out to get dinner.

I took him to Chuck E. Cheese's, and then we ran into the Galleria Mall for a little while to look around. As we were leaving the Galleria Mall, coming past the hotel that is attached to the Galleria Mall, I saw my husband, Truce, with another man at the hotel counter, all booed up.

I was stunned. I didn't say anything and went home. Truce came home around midnight and said that he had been working on a special project for the church. I said, "Okay, I understand!" I thought, *If it had been one of his past girlfriends or his last wife, I could have taken it better, but he was seeing a man.*

The Whispers

The whispers started. I knew because when I would walk up to a group of women or men for that matter, the atmosphere would change; and they would make sure they would mention something about church, Jesus, or even me or Truce Jr. I felt sick within my soul because this was a whole new territory for me that I knew nothing about, and I didn't know what to do.

One evening, as we were sitting in our spacious den, I said, "Truce, is everything okay?"

He said, "Yes, why do you ask?"

"Well, you appear to be really preoccupied these days, and we don't spend a lot of time together anymore. Have I done something?"

"No, Prada, there is just a lot of work to be done at the church."

I wanted to tell him about the *whispers*, but I just couldn't do it. I didn't know how to do it. And even if I mentioned it, he would deny it, even though I saw him. And I could never let him know that.

By Nature, Men Love Sex, and Women Love Men

I started to get confused. As a woman, I had always known that men love sex, and women love men. But I could not fathom that men loved men, which could carry over into sexual relationships. And even if it was written about in books, how could this be my real world? What am I to do about this? This was no longer a regular husband-and-wife situation but a pastor-and-wife situation, which I thought not to be normal.

Lace Up

I had always gotten a lot of attention because I was a teacher and a pastor's wife, so I kept an audience of some sort. However, I felt a change in the book club that I was a part of. I felt that way when I walked in the room because the atmosphere changed. I felt that they were against me because I had married this pastor, and maybe he had "touched" some of them before.

I decided to leave this book club and join another one where I knew none of the ladies. This change helped me so much as I was going through my journey with Truce. I had to do something. It was time for me to lace up.

Truce and I had only one child; and he was about to go off to college, so I had to do something. I decided to reverse what most wives would have done—confront him about the situation. I did not. I became his "butter roll." Yes, I was the pastor's wife, but I was about to put it on him this time like nobody's business.

I called Truce at church on Tuesday around 2:00 p.m. and said, "I need you to get somebody to preach on Sunday. I have special plans just for you. You have been working so hard, and I am taking you on vacation. I will not take no for an answer. Our flight leaves on Friday at 6:00 a.m. We are headed to Puerto Rico, and I already have your bags packed."

Truce said, "Well, all right!"

Friday came, and the plans went as planned. Upon arrival, Prada was going to show him who she really is!

Job Well Done

As soon as we hit the front door of the Rico Condominiums in Puerto Rico, I gave my all to Truce. "Truce, sit down and leave the rest to me." I slid off my dress and had on my birthday suit. I blindfolded Truce and then grabbed the anointing oil out of our Gucci luggage bags. "Truce, I am about to take you on a trip around the world, and when I finish, I know that you are going to say, 'Job well done!'"

I Do, I Do

"Truce, when we married twenty-three years ago, you said, 'I do,' to the preacher. Well, today, I am saying I do, I do. In other words, do I still love you after all these years? My answer is yes, Truce, and I need to know if you still love me?"

Truce didn't know what to say. After a few minutes, he looked at me and said, "You know that I do. You know that I do! I do, I do! We are in Puerto Rico, Prada. Let's please have some fun! And fun we do!"

We lay out on the sand and looked at the ocean. We also walked through the sand, and we made love morning, noon, and night!

If You Strive for Perfection, You Will Come Close

I felt that it was up to me to keep our marriage running smoothly. I had heard that if you strive for perfection, you will come close, and that is what I wanted for my marriage to this pastor—a marriage made in heaven!

After the beautiful weekend in Puerto Rico, we made our way back on Tuesday evening. As soon as we got back, Truce said that he needed to go by the church. I said, "I will be waiting for you, so hurry back."

I Dominate Because I Know Who I Am

I had a strong sense of my being. I knew that I had it going on!

I didn't doubt that fact, and that was why Truce chose me. As you could see, I would dominate because I knew who I was in whatever setting I was in. And the first time Truce and I met, I knew instantly that if I wanted him, he would be mine.

I was getting older, and I knew that I had to keep up. Truce was getting older too, but I didn't let him know that. He continued to work hard. The church was growing, and Truce Jr. was about to graduate from the Art Institute of Houston. We had come just about full circle in our marriage.

Then another incident happened like the one that had happened earlier. One night, Truce and I were watching a movie. When it ended, I told Truce I was going to bed. "Sweet dreams," he said, as I went to our bedroom. A couple of hours later, around 1:00 a.m. in the morning, I was awakened by the noise.

I got up to see what it was and noticed Truce was not in bed. I quietly went into the den, and there he was on the phone, talking to someone and arousing himself. I did not want to confront him, and I was too stunned, so I decided to go back to bed and go to sleep. I never said a word.

Seasons of a Woman

I decided to take stock of me. What was it about me that would make my husband, Truce, be attracted to other women or even men? I started questioning myself. As a woman, of course, I knew that women go through the changes of premenopause, menopause, and postmenopausal, which cause a number of mental symptoms, such as stress, anxiety, and mood swings. These changes could even make you think you were crazy.

But I had enough sense and education to take care of that and put it in check. As a woman, I knew the seasons of a woman, so I knew who I was and knew that I was not going to live my last days being unhappy with what had apparently been going on for years.

I wanted love, love, and love. I had had sex, sex, and more sex, and I had a good life. However, I could not deal with the trust issue I lately experienced in the game. It was killing me.

Now or Later

Truce and I had been married now for twenty-eight years. It was now 2003. It had become a heavy burden on me to stay or leave. As the days went on and with him changing more and more into womanizing and menanizing (if that's a word),

I had a decision to make. I felt that if I stayed in the marriage, I would die sooner than later. However, if I left the marriage, I still had about thirty or so more years to be happy and even remarry. Our relationship was no longer a "love relationship" but just a relationship alone.

I Am a Diamond

I didn't want to leave my marriage, but I had too because I knew that I was a jewel—a diamond! I would always look in the mirror and say to myself at my lowest point, "Prada, you are a diamond!" You see, a jewel is a precious stone that is smoothed and polished for use as an ornament. And that was exactly what Truce told me the night we met at the Christmas party, and I never forgot it. I was his diamond for his use in our marriage, and I accepted that. I didn't dare think that he wouldn't wear me all the time.

I was in whatever shape he needed me to be: round, princess, pear, heart, emerald, marquis, radiant, or oval. He called me his brilliant diamond, and I liked that! Why, because the brilliant diamond consists of fifty-eight facets in just one diamond, meaning whatever direction you look at it, it shines. And as his wife, I knew that I was shining. I knew that I was expected to go out and shine and sparkle and dazzle with the love that my husband had given me.

I knew that my stock as a "diamond wife" had gone up, but I also knew when my stock had dropped.

My *Swag!*

On December 15, 2003, I gave the speech of a lifetime to my husband, Truce, of twenty-eight years. It was the Christmas season: the Christmas trees were up all over Houston, Texas; the parties were starting; children were excited that Santa Claus was coming to town, the stores were buzzling, and everybody seemed so happy, but me. My swag was gone, and my it was what got me everything in life that I wanted. When Truce came home, I said, "Sit down. I got something to tell you."

"What is it, Prada? It seems like something has really upset you?"

"Yes, some. Truce, I have tried for so many years to be the best I could be for you, our family, and the church, but somehow you weren't satisfied."

"Prada, what are you talking about? I am satisfied! I have always been satisfied. Why are you doing this to me at Christmas time?"

"Truce, because I can't go into another year knowing that you lust after other women and men. We never had the problems that a lot of mixed couples have because I believed that you truly loved me and you may even still do. But in my heart, I can no longer accept your lifestyle. I put up with it for many years. I stopped saying anything to you about it because you would always say that I was imagining things, but Truce, I wasn't. I saw you at the hotel with a man years ago. I heard you on the telephone when you thought I was asleep, and I saw the things you were doing to yourself late at night.

"Truce, I know that you love me, and I love you, but I have to leave this marriage now for my sanity. I will always love you! We had many great years. You always took care of me, but I wanted to be the only one you loved other than God, and I realized for years that I wasn't the only one. I am leaving because my heart is telling me too. I can no longer take the hurt and distrust from you."

From Loving to Leaving

"The strong love that I had for you is gone. And the strong love that I had for myself is almost gone. Truce, I have found myself going from loving to leaving. Do you remember that song by Candi Staton, "Young Hearts Run Free?" There is a line in that song that says, "Don't be no fool when love really don't love you. Truce you will always be a part of me, but it's time for me to leave this marriage."

"Prada, don't leave me! Don't walk away!"

"Truce, I wish you the best, but I'm out! Merry Christmas, Baby!"

CHAPTER 3

Swinging the Wrong Way

*A*RE YOU PREPARED for the ride of your life? There were so many great songs in the 1980s like "When Doves Cry" by Prince, "All Night Long" by Lionel Richie, "Beat It" by Michael Jackson, and "Sexual Healing" by Marvin Gaye. As a white woman, I loved soul music.

As I was driving down Peachtree in Atlanta, Georgia, when I was nineteen years old in 1982, I never dreamed I would be where I am today! Here is my story. My name is Brandi Ghist, and my husband's name is Calvin Happi. Calvin was in the band at Georgia State, and I was studying theater at Georgia State. He was twenty-one.

One day between classes, Calvin saw me sitting in the student lounge. He came over to where I was, saying, "Hello. Is anyone sitting in that chair?"

I said, "No. You can sit there."

Calvin immediately sat down and started telling me all about himself and how he wanted to be a big star in the music industry. He wanted to be as big as Prince in the music industry.

"That's great, Calvin," I said. "Do you have any songs written that I can hear?"

He said, "Well, yes! As a matter of fact, I do."

I listened to one of his songs, and in that quick moment, I fell in love with him. I could not help myself. The feelings that he put in that one song took me to a place I had never been before.

I could not let him know how I felt because I was married. I had been married for thirteen months. My husband, Steve, and I had grown up together in the same neighborhood and had been childhood sweethearts. So naturally, we got married as soon as we were of age. But when I met Calvin, I couldn't help myself. I wanted him immediately.

What About Your Husband?

As time went on, Calvin and I became closer and closer. I had crossed over into adultery, but I didn't care. After sneaking around for two years, I decided that I wanted to leave my husband, Steve. I told Calvin of my plans to marry him. Calvin said, "What about your husband?"

"He will be okay," I said. "I can explain to him that we are still very young, and I know that he will heal in no time from the hurt of us parting ways."

One evening, when Steve got home, I said, "Steve, let's go to dinner so we can talk. I have something in my heart, and I must tell you about it."

Steve seemed very disturbed but said "Okay."

We each drove our own cars. We went to one of Atlanta's top restaurants. They serve the best handmade pansotti, which is a squash-filled pasta topped with an airy parmesan puff.

After we ordered our food and beverages and after we had eaten everything including desserts, I took another sip of my glass of red wine, Gamay, then said, "Steve, you know that I love you, right? And I will always love you, but I don't have the feelings for you like I used to. I have found someone else, and his name is Calvin. Please understand that it has nothing to do with you as a person, but I feel that I have truly found my soulmate."

Steve looked at me and said, "Brandi, you don't have to tell me but once. You can leave me, but just know that I will always love you too, boo!"

After we finished dinner, we drove back home in our separate cars, and I was on my way to love. I had a lot to do, starting with filing for divorce. It was easy because Steve and I didn't have any children, and we didn't have many bills since we were in school. Therefore, five months later, we were divorced.

Hustle

I had gotten the divorce. It was time for me to hustle! I was about to embark on a new life with a new man, a new marriage, and schoolwork. It was on!

Calvin and I did not have the typical wedding at a church. I didn't have time to have one at this moment in time. I was just ready to marry my soulmate, Calvin. As a matter of fact, we asked one of the professors at Georgia State to marry us in the student lounge on Friday, April 6, 1984. Everybody that could fit in the student lounge came. It was totally packed that day. And it was the most beautiful moment of my life. We were married at 1:00 p.m., and I became Mrs. Calvin Happi.

Swing Low

After Calvin graduated from Georgia State and with him being a musician, he would often stay out later than I thought he should. This was a new thing that I had to get used to. But I didn't care because I wanted him, and I got him. So whatever time he came home was fine with me until I found out why he often stayed out to around 6:00 a.m. three times a week. I was about to learn about Swing Low. I hired a private investigator, who followed Calvin for six months. I wanted to be very sure and to have good judgment on what would be revealed to me.

Well, I was not ready for this! I found out that Calvin was a swinger. He had been one before we got married and had just continued on through our marriage for twelve long years. The swingers club that he was a part of was also called the Lifestyle. This is a private club for single and married couples. He had not told me about it before we got married.

Since this was something way over my head, I researched it and found out according to the *USA* newspaper that approximately three to nine million people across the USA are members, which is about 15 percent of the population. They are doctors, lawyers, schoolteachers, parents. They are young, old, middle-aged, attractive, wealthy, interesting, churchgoing, and middle- to upper-class people. They even have conventions.

As I continued to investigate this lifestyle, I found out that the swingers are a group of people who loves to practice what's called swinging. Swinging is known as wife swapping or partner swapping where they engage in *sexual* activities as a social activity. This activity is carried on most weekends.

The swingers have private clubs all across the USA, even right here in Atlanta, Georgia. They are looking for fun and excitement! They often have parties with great music. They dance, they laugh and they have sex with someone other than their spouse. Often, the spouse is there at the party with someone else as well because it was agreed upon by both spouses.

As I continued to keep my mouth shut and researched this lifestyle, it was revealed that these kinds of parties would *replace* a love that's gone, commitment that's gone, and partner priority that's gone. In other words, he or she used to be the first place in a spouse's life.

They also engage in swinging because they want to be *happy* all the time. Studies show that couples in these kinds of arrangements tend to be happier and more satisfied in life. They participate in swinging so that their marriage won't get stale or they won't get hurt by a cheating spouse.

I even read where this club is considered to be an enhancement to marriage, but I thought it is a cop-out on marriage. I believe that everybody wants to be happy all the time, without the drama, but it is not realistic in marriage.

Having been married before, I knew that marriage would take work, and many couples wouldn't want to work hard at their marriage. They would work hard on their jobs but not on their marriages. And I realized that I had work to do on my new second marriage.

I had even read that 50 percent of marriages would end in divorce and the other 50 percent would engage in marital affairs. And yes, I believe that is true. I am a product of that statistics. But now this added thing called swingers was a part of my marriage, and I was about to have a major conversation with my husband, Calvin.

Do a Good Thing—Leave

After my discovery, what was I to do? Calvin and I had been married for twelve years. We did not have any kids because he was so busy traveling and making music. But once I discovered this new thing, I felt sick to my stomach. He never mentioned this side of his life to me. One night, when we were at home just chilling, I said, "Calvin, can we talk?" I had to get answers from him after I had done all the research and had paid the private investigator, which wasn't cheap. I just knew that I could not engage in that world.

Calvin said "Sure, darling, we can talk. What's up?"

"Calvin, I found out about your lifestyle, and I don't know what to do about it. Am I not enough for you?"

A Wife or Lover

"I am a wife to you and a lover. I know that you may think that I can only be one or the other, but I am both to you, Calvin. We have certainly had great times these twelve years, so why do you feel the need to continue to go to these kinds of places?"

"Brandi, none of that stuff means anything to me. I just like having some special kind of fun. It has nothing to do with you. You know that I love you!"

What Am I To Do?

"I know you do Calvin, but now that I know what's going on with you, how can I pretend that it is not happening? How can I not think that when you are away from home way into the early mornings that you are not swinging with others? Help me out, Calvin! What am I to do?"

I Had to Go

Calvin and I separated because he was not willing to stop the madness, and I could no longer accept his lifestyle. I had to go. I did not want my family back in Chicago to know what was going on. So I created this story about me having a new job, and I would have to leave Calvin. Since he was a musician, we would just commute back and forth. I had to get away and get myself together. I realized that I shared some of the blame because I was the aggressive one when we met. I took my share of the blame, but now what was I going to do about it?

Where Are We Going?

I went to Hartsfield-Jackson Atlanta International Airport and took a flight to Washington, DC, where I would live. I got a job as a vice president at Citibank. Once totally settled, I decided to write Calvin a letter instead of talking to him on the phone. I wanted to know what our future looked like. We had invested so many years, and I still loved him, but I knew that we would have to come to an understanding on our future.

I sat down at 9:20 p.m. on a Wednesday. I was feeling secure about what I was about to do. I started the letter with

"Calvin, where are we going?" I really needed to know the answer because I had left a husband before him, and I did not want that to happen again. We didn't have any children. We both had gotten a little older, and I needed to feel secure.

You Can't Get Away from Yourself

After I had written that five-page letter to Calvin, he responded back to me with a letter. (As you know, a letter sticks more to your soul than talking in person or on the telephone.) Calvin wrote about how when he was younger, he and his friends would do some strange, freaky things. "It was something that we could all participate in and have fun. It started around the age of nine and never stopped. The experience had become more enjoyable the more players that were involved in the game. It continued through middle school, high school, and college."

As I was reading Calvin's letter, my mind went back to when we first met and how I was the one who really wanted the relationship. So his final statement to me in the letter was "You can't get away from yourself." He was basically saying that it was who he was and that was that.

It's Time

Okay then, it was time. Let me start over. We had been married for twenty years, so let me leave that part of his life alone. If he honored and respected me, then I would just act as if that part of our marriage did not exist. Things got so much better after that conversation. I decided to move back home, and we carried on as husband and wife. We even bought a larger house because he was making more money as a producer of music, and I didn't have to work hard. We still did not have to worry about children because we were so involved in our careers.

I Will Do a New Thing

I decided that I would do a new thing. I went and got a shorter hairstyle. I lost ten pounds. (Not that I was heavy, but I wanted to look a little thinner.) I got a new wardrobe. I wanted Calvin to really want me like he would want the swingers. I never went with him to the swingers club even though he had asked me to on several occasions, but at least I could play the part in our marriage.

What's Love Got to Do with It?

Calvin always told me that he loved me, but I would wonder, *How could he? How could he so easily make love to two and three people at a time?* I even found out that Calvin was "swinging" with one of my best friends, Mercedes, whom I used to hang out with in college. One night, as we were sitting on the couch, watching a comedy show on News One, I asked him if he loved any of the women he had been with. His answer was "What's love got to do with it?"

Today It Ends

I believed my husband! I continued to carry on like nothing else was between us. We traveled all over the world because not only did he produce talented artists but he was also performing gigs himself. While we were in New Orleans for the Essence Festival, I started feeling sick. I was so sick until I thought I was pregnant. I had all the early morning sickness. My body was getting weaker and weaker.

When I collapsed in the hotel room, I was immediately taken to the emergency room. After staying there for three full days, it was discovered that I had contracted HPV (human papillomavirus). I asked the doctor, "What the hell is that?"

He told me it is a disease that is spread through sexual contact. He said, "It can be treated, but this condition cannot be cured. And it is chronic—meaning it can last for a lifetime."

I didn't have to think about who I had been with sexually in the last twenty-nine years because it had only been Calvin for as long as we had been married. I looked at Calvin because I knew where it came from. I said, "Though it has been twenty-nine years of marriage, today it ends, March 30, 2013."

After leaving the hospital, I also had to do my own research because this was a serious business. I read in *Seventeen* magazine an article on body and health. *Seventeen* magazine had been around for a very long time, actually since 1944, so I trusted what I was reading! The article I read was titled "What's Your STI-Q?" It talked about sexually transmitted infections that occur in the United States.

The article listed that people could get at least seven kinds of infection around the ages of fifteen to twenty-four years of age. They are pubic lice, HPV (human papillomavirus), HIV (human immunodeficiency virus), genital warts, gonorrhea, chlamydia, and herpes. The doctor was telling me I had HPV (human papillomavirus), meaning it could lead to cervical cancer. One can get it through oral, vaginal, and anal sex.

There's a vaccine to prevent it. For treatment, there is none, but the immune system clears up most cases within a year or two.

The Facts

The doctor had given me the facts. I loved this man so much, and he was about to kill me. I had this ungodly disease all because of love. How foolish was I to accept this death sentence years ago, all for the sake of love? Could I have not loved myself enough? I had a great future planned! I had a great education! Why did I allow myself to get out of myself?

Be True to Yourself

I went through the necessary treatments and got better. I went through counseling and got better! I wrote a letter to myself titled "Be True to Yourself" and got better. I moved into an apartment and got better! I attended a marriage Sunday school class called C.A.N.A. (Couples Achieving Newness Again) at the New Olivet Worship Center with my friend Chloe and got better. Calvin called me months later after he knew that I had gotten better. He would not accept the fact that our marriage was over. He thought I was just emotional when I said it to him in the hospital.

Since Calvin was a swinger and we married when I was only twenty-one and he was only twenty-three, I decided I was going to have some fun again! I started dating a younger man. I needed more and more love, and Calvin had stopped giving it to me. Calvin had a taste for women with big breasts, and though I did not have double Ds, I knew that I could work my big butt. I did that with Alex.

I started wearing tighter clothes that would highlight my butt. The women on my job noticed that I had changed. They became very jealous because they saw the attention that I was getting. They did not know why I had changed, and I could not let them know that I had become a "cougar" and that my marriage was ending because my husband was a swinger.

I left for Chicago because I found out that my mother was sick. I stayed with my mother for approximately two weeks. Calvin called me while I was there to check on me due to my own sickness and to check on my mother. I had gotten better, and my mother had gotten worse. But my family never knew what was going on with me. My mother had become ill, so much so that I was extremely worried.

She had cancer and did not tell me. She had been given six months to live. I was not prepared for this. After being home for just two weeks, my mother died. It broke my heart. I was trying to make her so happy with all my accomplishments because I knew that she was my biggest fan.

After I had the funeral for my mother, I went on with my way of living. I poured myself into my job, my marriage, and everything else that I was involved in. I wanted to make my mother—my number 1 fan—proud, and though she was gone, I felt her spirit. I wanted to remain sad, but I couldn't because she would not have wanted me to.

There was not a day that went by that I did not think of my mother. Even though, I was having a hard time in my marriage, I often wondered, *Would my mother be proud if I walked away from my marriage?*

When I got back in town, I knew what I had to do. I had wondered if my mother would be proud if I walked away from my marriage after twenty-nine years. The answer was yes because she walked away from hers much sooner than I.

I called Calvin. After a long ten minutes on the telephone, he would not accept the fact that our marriage was indeed over. He still thought I was just emotional. As we talked about many things, I finally said to him, "Be true to yourself, and because of my truth, the lie of our marriage is over. The divorce papers are in motion and should arrive to you soon."

Calvin still had the nerve to say, "Brandi, don't walk away!"

My answer was "Calvin, you swung away."

CHAPTER 4

Up from Here

THE YEAR WAS 1977 in Los Angeles, California—a place where a lot of pretty people live and where beautiful men and women come from all over the world, hoping to be discovered by some major TV show. I met Brent coming out of the Whole Foods Market. He was Hispanic just like me. He was built to the tee, if you will. He had this amazing six-pack body build. He had a tattoo of a sword that was amazing! I could not keep my eyes off him as he was walking past me going to his car. I was headed into the market. He noticed me as well when I walked by, but he only said "Hello."

As I went into the store, it was as if I was frozen. I couldn't move. I thought I would never see him again, but then he walked back in the store. He had forgotten to get a loaf of bread. Thank God! It was my opportunity to meet him before he walked out of the store again. (I had not even gotten my cart yet to get my own groceries.) "Hi, how are you? My name is Ciara. Ciara Wrothe. I saw you as you passed by earlier. I noticed you didn't have a wedding band on, so I assume you are not married. Here is my business card."

"Thank you, Ciara, and hi to you! My name is Brent Anthony Basby, and the reason I don't have a wedding band on is because I am not married."

You will later see how this story ends. Just know this, Ciara said, "Oh no, I'll never love this way again! Believe that!"

I'm Winning

I, Ciara, had to get help after loving this man so much. After meeting at the grocery store and Brent calling me two hours later that day, let me just say, the rest is history. At the time, he was thirty-three, and I was thirty. He is a fitness trainer at one of the top Fitness Centers in Los Angeles, and I am a dentist. We got married six months later in June of 1978 because I always wanted to be a June bride! My wish was granted.

I had heard that there is nothing like a June bride. June 5 was the day! It was so very special! I had my five best girlfriends—Terri, Sarah, Riley, Lea, and Nicole—and he had his five best guys—Cliff, Kent, Solomon, Joshua, and Carey. We got married at Solar Baptist Church in California at 4:00 p.m. Our colors were gray and teal. The bridesmaids wore teal, and the groomsmen wore gray tuxedos with teal trimmings. I could not be happier. We had written our own vows. Brent had a line that said, "I will forever be true to my sweet love, Ciara." And I had a line that said, "Whatever Brent wants from me, Brent will get." Brent wanted sex 24-7, and I gave him what he wanted.

We had our daughter, Majestic, a year later. I remember so clearly that day: Brent and I decided to go to the movies. We went to see Kramer vs. Kramer, which was getting rave reviews. It was about a wife leaving her husband and child, and I did not realize at the time just how close to home it would be. However, an hour into the movie at 2:00 p.m., my water broke, and panic was everywhere. "Someone, please call the paramedics!" shouted Brent. Once they arrived and got me settled, our little girl was born right there at the Majestic movie theater on June 19, 1979. We named her Majestic!

As the years passed, ten years at the time, things were going smoothly as husband and wife. One Friday night, we got into a heated argument, and Brent slapped the hell out of me. I saw stars! I could not believe it. I had not seen that side of him before. He had started drinking on a regular basis about a year ago. I knew that he had been very busy with clients at the fitness club, so I tried to blame his long hours for his tiredness and the need to drink more and more on his work schedule. However, the abuse became more and more frequent. My daughter and I would try to get out of his way and go to bed before he would come home. Sometimes it would work, and sometimes it would not.

Brent would come through the door, hollering at me, "Ciara, get up and fix me dinner!"

I shouted back, "Brent, I did and left it on the stove."

Brent hollowed again, "I don't want cold or warmed-over food. Get your ass up now, and fix me some hot food." As his normal routine, he would come and drag me out of the bed and hit me, often leaving several bruises on my body. I didn't know why, but I took this abuse for the next fifteen years. If it wasn't one thing, it was another thing that he would fuss and cuss about. After all those years of abuse, I knew I had to do something. I didn't want to tell anybody, but I finally realized that I was experiencing domestic abuse. I had to do something in a hurry! I had to tell my best friend, Sabrina, who would keep my daughter when I needed her to.

I went to a shelter for abused women to get help and safety, and then everything started to change. "Hello, my name is Ciara, and my husband beats me. Can you help me?"

"Yes, Ciara, we can," said Ms. Mabry, the social worker at the shelter.

On my very first week, I noticed a young lady in her early thirties looking at me, and then she turned away. I quickly looked at her and noticed that it was Terri, one of my very best friends who was in my wedding. "Terri, what are you doing here?"

She immediately said, "Ciara, what are you doing here?"

After we cried and talked for hours, we realized we had lost touch with each other because we were both ashamed of something that neither of us wanted—to be abused by our spouses and not loved. After that visit, we decided to stay in touch until things got better for both of us.

Twenty years passed, and I was no longer happy in my marriage. I had to try to find happiness in my troubled times. I read a book that stated, "Happiness is defined as the experience of joy, pleasure, satisfaction, cheerfulness, contentment, and positive well-being combined with a sense that one's life is good, meaningful, and worthwhile." I finally realized that when trouble times would come, not only one piece of happiness went away but all of it, and I felt it. I knew that if I did not do something, then I would loose big time, so I had to remind myself every day that I was winning!

Inside of Me

I had to ask myself many questions. I had to decide. Where would I go from this low place? Where would I go when love doesn't last? Where would I go when I thought we were destined to be married until death do us part? Where would I go after giving my body to him in love? Where would I go when I thought I was the only pretty woman to my husband, Brent?

The inside of me was dying until I got the answers. I had to go up from where I was and had to live my best life. So I decided to throw a party.

As a dentist, I would always invite people over for dinner parties. I loved the color burgundy, so I would always have everything decked out to match my burgundy oriental rug. I would have burgundy table clothes, plates, napkins, cups, and forks. I would even put a burgundy collar on my dog, Kodie. And this party was no different.

When my friend Kelly came over to my house for the first time to the party, she developed a very jealous spirit about herself, even stating things like, "Oh, you have two stoves? Who needs two stoves? Is that television big enough? Who needs a television that big? Why did you invite Zoe from News 5?" Well, what Kelly didn't know was that I had one too many drinks. One could say I was a borderline drunk.

I turned to Kelly and said, "Did you pay for anything in this house? I am having issues, and here you come with some nonsense about my house and you are living in an apartment complex." I did not even give her time to answer. I said, "Get your ass out of my house! This friendship ends now! Bye!"

Ciara greeted other guests and started having fun with all of them. She had a "thing" for good-smelling cologne, and so when she passed by her dental hygienist, John, and got a whip of his cologne, she already being somewhat drunk. When the music was jamming, she started dancing very provocatively with him. His cologne brought her closer to him than she should have been.

But at the same time, she was close enough to hear several women say "sweet nothings" to her husband, Brent, even with the loud music. Already drunk, she started cursing out all the women in attendance and then told everyone to leave. She shouted, "The party is over!"

After everyone left, she realized that she had made a fool of herself and that she had crossed the line with her friends. Because of the troubles in her marriage, she had started drinking more than socially. She had actually become an alcoholic just like her husband because of all the stress that Brent had put her through.

The next day, she went and got help because she knew that she was losing it, and she blamed Brent for what she had become. She knew that time had passed. She told her therapist, "We have been married for thirty years! Yes, thirty years. And now I realize that I should have left so many years ago."

I Got Educated

I decided to get smarter about my marriage. I wanted to really understand why I was getting abused and why my husband switched up. I started reading the books at the shelter when I had to go there. According to statistics, the number of domestic violence in most cities is on the rise.

In places like Memphis, a woman gets abused every single day of the year. I heard from a speaker at the shelter who spoke to us that there are *five* things an abused woman must do:

1. You must tell someone.

2. You must take positive action to get out of the situation because most of the times, it doesn't get any better.

3. You must have hope, remembering who you were before the abuse started, even as a little girl and the dreams you had. And then work to get it back.

4. You must get some kind of education or training or a skill where you won't have to be dependent on someone else for your survival in life.

5. Once you get out of that situation, you must be an advocate for others, especially young girls. They are getting younger and younger in terms of being abused.

I Am Keenly Aware

Here I was, married to this "fine" man, and instead of him catering to my needs, I was keenly aware that I was catering to his needs because I always went back in my mind as to when I first saw him and how I wanted him so badly. (Be careful what you ask for.)

Where Am I Going for the Future?

I had to get up! I started speaking out for abused women. I wrote monthly letters to the shelter when I wasn't in there. The letter would say something like "Hello, my friend [or *Hello, my sister*] I am thinking of you. I am praying for you, and I know things are going to get better. Sincerely, your friend." I knew how it would make them feel.

I kept on praying for the abused women because I did not want them to be a forgotten group. My friend Terri had received my letter at the shelter and called me one Monday morning. "Hi, Ciara, this is Terri. I received your beautiful letter, but I am still in the same situation years after we saw each other in the shelter. I just can't leave my husband. He really needs me." She never wanted to leave her husband, who was an alcoholic, because she thought she could help him.

As abused women, we don't often know what our future holds, so we try to hold on. But we can at least try and get up and then have an idea of where we are going for our future. I found my answer.

Spice Up

When Brent realized that I was changing after he was the one who was responsible for me going to the shelter, he really started straightening up. He then wanted to spice up our marriage. He went all in as to loving me again, respecting me, having sex with me, and everything else that I had come to enjoy.

Drop It, Leave It, and Let It Go

Could I really drop it, leave it, and let it go? He had done horrible things to me for so many years like chasing me and our children in the storm late one night to our neighbor's house, hollering at us the whole time. How embarrassing was that? Could I really let go of how he cussed me flat out in front of his family at a family reunion when I just asked him if he was ready for me to cut the cake?

You Crushed My Spirit

"Brent, I know I am a little slow at loving you again and doing the things that I used to do for you early in our marriage, but you crushed my spirit. Please allow me time to heal and get over all the hurt. I am trying to forget the pain you have caused our family and yourself. You see, I have found that abuse is like running water. It never stops! It continues to drip, drip, and drip. And with that newfound revelation, it is going to take me some time to get back to normal."

You're Tripping

Brent shouted at me, "Ciara, what are you talking about? You're tripping!"

I shouted back, "Are you serious, Brent? Did you say I am tripping? Well, I be damned! You have given me blue eyes. You almost snatched all my hair out until I was almost bald-headed on one side. You had me living in fear for many years. You would tell me about the other women who you said gave you better sex than me and then when I would cook for you, you would often say, 'I am not hungry!' And now you say I am tripping?"

I Am Slayed but Looking Good

I knew I was looking good when I was talking to Brent. I felt his eyes were over me. I knew he wanted to make love to me at that moment, but I knew that I couldn't. I knew in my heart that I had checked out of the marriage. For the many years that he had abused me and our daughter and embarrassed me, I could no longer live like that. I had become educated enough to know that if I stayed, I might not live.

The Longevity of Marriage

When Brent and I married, I just knew that it would last forever. Even after ten years of abuse, I kept hoping it would get better. Then another ten years went by, and then another. It added up to thirty years of abuse. How could I stay in such a situation for so long? Who was I? When a light bulb went off in my head for real, I realized the longevity of my marriage to Brent, then I said, "Not anymore!"

I Was Married

As a woman, I allowed a man to take everything good away from me. Was I dreaming? Did this really happen? There were so many men in the world, and I saw only one. What planet did I come from? Yes, I was married, but I was also in denial about a lot of things. The song by the singer Michael Bolton and so many others says, "When a man loves a woman, / he can't keep his mind on nothing else. / He'd trade the world for a good thing he's found." I apparently wasn't that woman.

How Dare You

When I finally woke up, came to my senses, and realized that I had been taken advantage of as a wife, I said to Brent, "How Dare You? How dare you take thirty years of my life? You are not even God, but somehow you thought you were. As a matter of fact, you really don't know who you are. And I don't know who you are. We have lived a fake life all these years, but you know what Brent—"

Not Business as Usual

"It is no longer business as usual. I have got to spend the rest of my days on a new trajectory. I still have hopes and dreams for my life, and if only I believe, I can get there. I thank you for listening, and now after thirty years, I will experience freedom again. The divorce papers will arrive to you in three days on Friday. I have to go *up* from here."

Thirty Whole Years

"Brent, as you know, from growing up in church, there is a story in the Bible about how Jesus was crucified on a Friday, but on the third day, he got up with all power. Well, I am using his example. I got up! And in the same Bible, I know you know this story as well how the Israelites wandered in the wilderness for forty years waiting for the Promised Land. It has been thirty whole years for me, and I can't go another ten. I am getting up from here too! I am leaving the wilderness!

"After spending thirty whole years with you and suffering most of them, I decided to tell someone about my abuse. I told those in authority at the shelter what you had done to me and our child. Not only that, but I started helping the women at the shelter to get up from that place of hate.

"The year 2008 brought about a lot of changes for us, and so today at the age of sixty and after thirty whole years, I decided that I must go up from here. I don't want to stay in the wilderness any longer. I won't take it anymore!"

"Ciara, please. Baby, please, don't walk away!"

Ciara looked Brent in his eyes and said, "Brent, my love, the divorce papers are on the way. Thirty whole years is long enough."

CHAPTER 5

Goodbye!

"Now unto him that is able to do exceeding abundantly above all that we ask or think, according to the power that worketh in us"
—King James Version (KJV)

LUCAS AND I, Olivia, were married on Thanksgiving on November 26, 1991. I had hit the big forty. He was forty-five. It was the best day of our lives, so I thought. We both had been in previous relationships. His relationship was steady, and mine was not. He had been dating Lena for five years and had planned to get married, and I had been dating Sidney for two years with no plans of marriage. Both of our careers had taken us all over the world. I was an administrator for charter schools, and he was a bond attorney. And while relationships were important to us, marriage wasn't.

He Won't Stop *Looking*

It was Friday, February 8, 1991. I was at a banquet for the Soulsville Charter School at the Peabody Hotel in Memphis, Tennessee, where I lived. As I got settled in my seat, the program began with a prayer given over the event and a prayer given over the food. When the prayer ended, I looked up, and there he was. This man at the next table was smiling at me like a Cheshire cat. I acknowledged him and kept eating and talking to those at the table where I was seated.

No matter how many times I would look up or around, there he was smiling at me! I was thinking, *What is wrong with this man? How can he be so attentive to me when his date or supposed-to-be bride (she had what looked like an engagement ring on) is sitting right next to him?*

As the program progressed, I got up from my seat to go out to the ladies' bathroom. When I came out of the bathroom, there he was still smiling as a Cheshire cat again. He spoke and said, "You have got to be the most beautiful woman here. What is your name?"

Of course, I was flattered because there were over five hundred people there and many women, and for him to say that I was the most beautiful one there, well, I am just saying! I said, "Well, thank you!"

He said, "What is your name?"

"Olivia Dream," I said. I then asked him, "What is your name?"

"My name is Lucas Napin."

I went on to say, "Aren't you here with someone, Lucas?"

He said, "Yes, but what does that mean? I see you and you only."

Well, that was enough for me because my boyfriend had never expressed that kind of excitement about my beauty. Lucas and I exchanged telephone numbers right there in the beautiful Peabody lobby. I then went back into the event, and five minutes later, he came back in and sat next to his girlfriend while watching me the whole time.

When I got home around 10:30 p.m. that night, he called me. He told me all about himself, and I told him all about me. He told me I looked very familiar because he had been at a beach in Saint Lucia several months ago, and he thought he had seen me there. *Well, yes, he had!*

He said that he saw me in a bathing suit that took his breath away. That was when I had gone to Saint Lucia with some girlfriends in July of 1990. And he was right! I was there. And now seven months later in February, fate brought us together in Memphis, Tennessee—the home of the best music in the world, from Isaac Hayes to Elvis Presley, Justin Timberlake, Aretha Franklin, Kirk Whalum, Kenneth Whalum III, Kortland Whalum, Kameron Whalum, Kevin Whalum, Ralph White and so many more. He couldn't wait to talk to me and learn more about me. We stayed on the phone for hours until 4:00 a.m.

Lucas would not leave me alone! He called me every single day, all day long. He did not want to lose me after seeing me again. He could call when he wanted too because he was the managing partner in a huge law firm, and therefore, he could run his own schedule. He would also come to Memphis on weekends to see me. It was really getting pretty serious. One weekend, he drove his red corvette to Memphis! When I saw the car pull up to my house, I thought it was the singer Prince. Lucas said, "Don't say a word. Just get in the car."

He was jamming to Beyonce's "Crazy in Love." The song started with "You Ready?" I thought, *Well, yes, I am!* So there we were, all hugged up, and we took off down the street.

After his flattery won me over, we started hanging out a lot. He then popped the question to me on April 5, 1991, after dinner one night in his hometown in Boston. He asked me to marry him! Without hesitation, I agreed when he gave me a five-carat princess diamond ring after two months of meeting him.

New Beginnings

That ring did it for me! There was only one problem—his mother. She did not know me, and I did not know her. They lived in Boston, and I lived in Memphis. You know, sometimes North and South don't mix. After visiting Boston and meeting her, I saw her vibe. She thought I was competing with her for her son, but her son was competing with other men for me. She was nowhere in the picture as far as I was concerned.

We married on Thanksgiving Day, Thursday, November 26, 1991. All our families were able to attend during the holiday in Memphis. Lucas did not spare anything! He gave me everything I wanted and then some. It was the most beautiful and perfect wedding I could imagine. It was about to be a new beginning for this couple who just happened to meet while in the company of their own significant other.

My Promised Land

We settled in New York City, where most of the major law firms were. I continued to work for charter schools. Our lives merged with ease. Lucas left the law firm as managing partner and opened his own law firm specializing in bond financing. He continued to make more and more money in his new law firm. My promised land started with Lucas giving me everything that I ever wanted. Life was so good!

I was able to live the high life going to my favorite stores like Gucci, Louis Vuitton, Barneys New York, Lord & Taylor, Bloomingdale's, Saks, Goyard, and all other major stores. It was so amazing! I still thought that it could not get any better. We would often go to the Broadway theaters on weekends. After living in a penthouse for a year, Lucas bought me the most beautiful house close to Central Park so that when I got pregnant and had our children, I could take them to the park.

Our new house was also close to New York City Charter School Center where I worked. One day, when two of my coworkers and I had finished lunch and shopping, they asked to see my new home because I had talked about it so much being near Central Park.

They wanted to see the turquoise curtains that I had in the game room where the pool table was turquoise too. I obliged and took them to my new home. They loved everything about it. After an extended lunch and two hours later, we made it back to work.

For the rest of the day and two solid weeks, they avoided me. Unfortunately, they had become jealous of how well I was living. Just like that, they did not want me in their circle, but I was not surprised because it was the same thing that my cousins, Mary and Joyce, did. They became extremely jealous of the way I was doing it—Big Willie Style. What they did not realize was that I was used to that reaction from others.

Several years prior, when I had my birthday party at the famous Peabody Hotel in Memphis, many of those whom I invited free of charge were so jealous of my celebration that I actually saw smoke coming from their nostrils. But I was married to this bond attorney who had it like that, and he got me what I wanted. And I was not going to apologize for it!

So after assessing that situation with coworkers, I moved on from them and continued my work and continued enjoying life with my new husband. I continued to enjoy our beautiful home near Central Park in New York. I continued to get it ready for when I would become pregnant. However, after trying to have a baby many times, it was determined that I could not have children.

One evening, when he was home early, I told him I needed to speak with him. "Lucas, do you know how much I love you?"

"Yes, I do, Olivia, but you can show me." He wanted to make love right then.

"Lucas, okay, later, but I have something very important to say. I went to the doctor and found out that I cannot have children. I have been diagnosed with infertility. I am not ovulating. Please forgive me because I know how badly you want two sons."

Lucas said, "Olivia, I understand. We apparently can't do anything about it, so we will adopt. We can adopt one baby boy, and once you get situated and adjusted, we can adopt a second one when you are ready. How does that sound?"

"Lucas, thank you so much for making that easy for me. I will start the process tomorrow." I wanted to give Lucas what he wanted. He always wanted two boys, so what if they were to be adopted?

If That's What It Takes

I was able to grant him his request. We adopted Lucas Jr. six years later on April 7, 1997. Then on August 10, 1999, our second adopted son, Alexander, came into our lives. We welcomed each of our sons at six weeks old. If that was what my new husband wanted and if I wanted his continued love, then I had no problem giving him what he asked for.

My husband continued to love me, adore me, and give me the world, and I was going to give him my very best in our marriage, especially since we started our lives together later in age.

The New Porn—Social Media

The new porn—social media—had become the new norm in America in early 2000. Lucas and I started communicating a lot that way. He spent lots of time on Facebook, Snapchat, Instagram, and Twitter, looking at different posts. He would email me or text me all day long instead of calling me like he used to. He was still telling me how much he loved and adored me even with a lot of my attention going toward our two sons who kept me quite busy. This new way of communicating was actually okay with me because it was quick and easy. And I was okay with that because we did not want anything more! Lucas really took care of us.

His routine schedule of leaving home around 7:00 a.m. and returning home around 11:00 p.m. kept going and going. Now years later, with two teenagers, it was starting to be a bit much. When I mentioned it to Lucas, he said he would get me a nanny.

My thoughts were "a nanny? Your sons need you and I do too, at least sometimes!"

One night in 2003, I couldn't sleep, so I decided to get on the computer to browse on the internet. Let me tell you, I was not ready for what I saw. My husband, Lucas, had been looking at porn all day long on the computer before he went to work. I was sure he also did that when he was at work and when he got home!

I became confused! How could he do this to me when he consistently told me how he loved me and how I was the most beautiful woman? I felt so hurt and so betrayed.

When he got home, I confronted him and asked him about it. He could not lie because all the evidence was in my face and in his face. "Lucas, what is wrong?"

"Nothing," he said. "It is just that I have been looking at porn for many, many years."

When Lucas said that, my mind went back to that moment when he was telling me how he saw me in that swimsuit in Saint Lucia before we even met back in Memphis, Tennessee. I then realized that he had a problem with bare skin or nearly naked women. I knew that Lucas loved the "sight" of beautiful naked women. He loved looking at them so much until he bought five pairs of colored shades to look at them on his computer.

Go Figure

I had an Oprah "aha" moment! I had to go figure this out! How could my world be falling apart with this man who I had fallen in love with and who had given me everything I had ever dreamed of? I wanted and did adopt two babies for him, and that was not good enough. What was I going to do? I could not live with the feeling of betrayal in my marriage.

The Fight

I decided that I would not give up on my marriage and that I would give it the fight of its life. I went to counseling with Lucas because I knew that it was a real problem. And I was not about to let a *machine* (a computer) wreck my family. Lucas stayed in marriage counseling for more than three months. He was doing so much better, and we continued with our married life of happiness and wholeness.

I did everything I could to convey to Lucas that there was no way to live in fantasy with another woman, especially on the internet. He wasn't some young school boy, so I knew that he knew better. But he needed to be held accountable, and I was going to handle that.

Well, That's a Wrap!

When Lucas Jr., who was a junior at Golden State University, and Alexander, who was a freshman at Virginia State University, went off to college, I knew that I had to change my game and get more attentive to Lucas like I used to. When he would arrive home around 11:30 p.m. at night and open the door, I would be standing there naked. (That is what he was used to when he looked at porn.) "Hello, Lucas! You know that I can have a party anytime I want, and you are always invited."

Lucas with his eyes bucked said, "Well, thank you, my love! I am ready for the celebration too, with whipped cream please!"

Also, in the mornings, when he would take his shower, I would tag along in the shower as well. He really enjoyed me in those moments. He would often say, "Olivia, will you wash my back?"

I would answer, "Of course, I will, and when I finish, will you wash mine?"

"Olivia, don't play! I will be happy too!"

This new way of loving him was short-lived. Unfortunately, it didn't last long at all. One night, he left one of his cell phones at home and had gotten about fifty sexual texts and emails from women all over the world. They knew that he was this big time attorney making big money.

They even knew he was married to me but did not care. They just wanted him to "want" them individually. They would show every part of their bodies to this married man. And this married man apparently enjoyed it very much! It was so much so that he would answer each one back with his different names like Big Juice, Supreme, Pepper, Flex, and Salty.

Beat Your Ass

When Lucas, Big Juice, Supreme, Pepper, Flex, and Salty, all wrapped up in one man, got home, I beat his ass! I beat the daylight out of him. He had never seen that side of me, and I had not either.

Where Is the Love?

As I was beating him, I asked him, "Where is the love you said was mine, / all mine until the end of time? / Was it just a lie? / Where is the love? / If you had had a sudden change of heart, / I wish that you would tell me so. / Don't leave me hanging on the promises. / You've got to let me know. / Oh, how I wish I never met you. / I guess it must have been my fate to fall in love with someone else's love. / All I can do is wait. / That's all I can do.

"Yes, Lucas, I am giving you the lyrics of the song by Roberta Flack because what you have done to me is insane, and I just couldn't think on my own."

Turn Me Lose

Turn me lose, Olivia! Stop beating me! My head is bleeding! My back is hurting. I have lost my two front teeth, but I do love you! I didn't lie about my love for you."

"Really, Lucas? Stop lying, Lucas!" I said as I smacked him across his head.

"Rebecca, you know I don't love those porn stars. I just have a bad habit."

"Rebecca? My name is Olivia, you idiot! Yes, you do have a bad habit, Lucas, if you called me one of your porn friends' names. I can't deal with it anymore!"

Since Lucas stayed preoccupied during the day and later at night, I decided I would go to a charter school conference in Miami for four days. I met so many wonderful people, including Mr. McKenzie. He and I became friends in such a short time. He was an administrator for the charter schools in Miami. He was such a lovely man, and when he invited me to his home for dinner, I accepted it on the last day of the conference, which was Friday night, because I was leaving that Saturday morning.

I assumed he was married because he had a wedding band on and wanted me to meet his wife.

To my surprise, when we arrived at his home, no one was there. He led me into the den. As we sat and talked about the conference, I assumed that his wife had gone out to get the dinner before we got there. But that was not the case. He asked me if he could kiss me. I was totally shocked and said, "No! I am married!"

"But that does not matter." He told me his wife was out of town, and he had free reign. He pulled me close! He strong-armed me, and he yanked my clothes off and began to kiss me all over my body.

I fought, hollered, and screamed, but to no avail. He lived in a gated community that was spread out, and no one would ever hear me. He took what he wanted. We had sex for the next thirty minutes. Afterward, he took me back to the conference building. I had to get my own taxi to go to my hotel. I could not tell anyone because I was supposed to be intelligent enough to not let anything like this happen to me.

Even though I was angry at my husband, Lucas, for how he was not paying me any attention, I did not welcome the advances of Mr. McKenzie, and I did not want this to happen to me. I made it back to my hotel. Then I made it back to New York to my beautiful home, and I never mentioned it.

As time went on, I read an article on the #MeToo movement by Robin Western in the *AARP* magazine dated July 25, 2018. For forty years, Robin refused to confront one of the worst moments in her life. But I couldn't wait that long! I wanted to tell someone that I had been taken advantage of, but I couldn't join that movement.

I knew that I was taken advantage of because you could spot a mile away the sadness that I carried around with me. I was vulnerable. I was taken advantage of because my husband was no longer loving me like I thought he should.

No Capacity for Love

I had no more capacity for love. After that trip to Miami, I confronted Lucas. I said, "I want a divorce!"

"What?" exclaimed Lucas. "After twenty-seven years of marriage and all that I have done for you, you can't deal with this small issue of mine. Are you kidding me? Didn't I give you everything you want?"

A Man Has Got to Be a Man

"Olivia, a man has got to be a man! Think about all of the famous men who were married and have gotten in trouble with other women. They loved their wives! Olivia, but a lot of men cheat. They can't help it! It is in their DNA!"

He Used to Be My Guy

Am I stupid, or what, to accept my husband's explanation of cheating? True enough some women would accept it and go on living with the cheater, but my heart would not let me. If I stayed in this marriage, the act of infidelity would be a part of my world for the rest of my life, stopping my growth. I would not accept that! My life was bigger than one man. I was sixty-seven years old. I was in the second half of my life, and there was possibly a third life span. I planned to get there happily!

Nothing Else to Say

"Lucas, I love you so much that I have to leave. After twenty-seven years of marriage, I thank you! Lucas, I still have many years ahead of me, and I am not going to linger on the past. Lucas, do you remember the song by the late Aretha Franklin? If you want a do-right-all-day woman, you've got to be a do-right-all-night man. Lucas, with that said, I will remember the good times we had, but now, you have made me look forward to *owning* my own life. My attorney will be in touch with your attorney, unless you represent yourself! I have nothing else to say but *goodbye*!"

AUTHOR'S NOTE

THERE'S AN OLD saying "If you treated your wife the way you treated your hooker, you'd have the world's strongest marriage" (Bob Larkin, "What Escorts Can Teach a Married Man," *Men's Health*, November 2016).

Let's just say America is a divorcing nation. Just about every state has a double-digit divorce rate. Reason after reason is given as to why a spouse must leave a spouse. But wait, even after being married for more than twenty-five years?

Aren't there benefits for being married so long? Statistics continues to show so many famous people in particular, especially married men, whose wives give great reasons as to why they should leave their husbands. Husbands are often told to "enjoy your fantasies, but don't act on it" (Bob Larkin, "What Escorts Can Teach a Married Man," *Men's Health,* November 2016).

But wait again, it seems a lot of men are the same, and they continue to do the same thing over and over, which often leads to their divorce. Could it be heredity from the beginning of time? Could it just be in their DNA?

Could a wife just overlook her husband's sinful nature and see the good in him, especially if she has already stayed for twenty-five plus years? She often asks herself, "Am I to continue to help this husband of mine after all these years if I have already stayed at least twenty-five years?" Didn't the Bible say a wife is a helpmeet? That means she has a lot to help with, even her husband's way of living.

The final decision is yours, wives. Ann, Prada, Brandi, Ciara, and Olivia made their decision. They decided to leave their marriages after more than twenty-five years. No one can tell you to leave a spouse or not. You know the circumstances. Only your heart can tell you. "The shock of finding that you aren't loved is the deepest cut" (AARP / my favorite Beatles song / Rosanne Cash). Often, a wife who leaves her husband can go on and accomplish many great things, or she can suffer the consequences.

Also, a wife who decides to stay in her marriage can go on and accomplish so many great things (e.g., the first lady Hillary Clinton). She chose to stay in her marriage after President Bill Clinton's public infidelity. She then served as the sixty-seventh United States Secretary of State under President Obama from 2009 to 2013, overseeing the department that conducted the foreign policy of Barack Obama. After that, she ran for president of the United States again in 2016 against President Trump. For her, she made the right decision with her heart. She stayed in the marriage and focused on her own agenda as well. She and Bill Clinton recently met the beautiful young singer Ariana Grande—nothing but smiles from both of them. They have been married for forty-three years (October 11, 1975) through the ups and downs of marriage.

Also, to keep their marriage fresh and up-to-date, the Obamas—former president Obama and former first lady Michelle—attended the concert of the beautiful Beyonce. From the look of things, both enjoyed it equally. I am sure it spiced up their love life. Research shows them jamming and dancing while attending the concert. The Obamas celebrated twenty-six years of marriage on October 3, 2018.

You can still be the wife, but you may want to act like and dress like the girlfriend you used to be to your husband if that is what it takes. Twenty-five years and more of a special marriage union is a whole lot of life to give up!

ABOUT THE COUPLES
(Tyde, Nelson, Happi, Basby, and Napin)

1. **The Tydes**

   Pierre Tyde and Jenny Ann Brussel (Black couple)

   Ages eighteen and nineteen

   Married on Valentine's Day in 1959

   Nashville, Tennessee

   Have two children named Samuel and Anna Rose and

   a cat named Bloomingdale

   Carpenter/housewife

   Met while Jenny Ann was walking down the street

   Married for twenty-six years

   His problem—he liked prostitutes

2. **The Nelsons**

   Truce Nelson and Prada Yoke (Mixed Couple- Truce is white & Prada is black)

   Ages twenty-three and twenty-six

   Married in August in 1976

   He had been married before

   Houston, Texas

   Have one son, Truce Jr.

   Pastor/teacher

   Met at Christmas Party

   Married for twenty-eight years

   His problem—he liked women and men

3. **The Happi's**

   Calvin Happi and Brandi Ghist (White couple)

   Ages twenty-three and twenty-one

   Married in April 1984

   Atlanta, Georgia

   No children

   Students at Georgia State (he was in a band / she was studying) Theater

   Met at Georgian State College

   Married for twenty-nine years

   His problem—he was a swinger

4. **The Basbys'**

   Brent Basby and Ciara Wrothe (Hispanic couple)

   Ages thirty-two and thirty

   Married in June 1978

   Los Angeles, California

   Have one daughter, Kristen

   Fitness trainer / dentist

   Met at Whole Foods Market

   Married for thirty years

   His problem—he was an alcoholic and abuser

5. **The Napins'**

   Lucas Napin and Olivia Dream (Black couple)

   Ages forty and forty-five

   Married in November on Thanksgiving in 1991

   New York (She was from Memphis, and he was from Boston)

   Have two adopted sons, Lucas Jr. and Alexander

   Bond attorney / administrator for charter schools

   Met at a banquet for Soulsville in Memphis, Tennessee

   Married for twenty-seven years

   His problem—he was a social media junkie of porn

EPILOGUE

(Wisdom from Older Men)

1. When an older man likes very young girls, he is caught up in the change of life but really doesn't realize what he is doing. He just knows he is still a man and wants to keep whatever kind of appeal he had when he was a young boy.

2. It's in the medicine why some men change. Viagra, blood pressure, or any other kind of medicine, and often alcohol helps men to cope, which sometimes lead them to being alcoholics.

3. A woman must wait until her man gets caught before she takes any action. If he never gets caught, she has nothing to worry about.

4. A lot of marriages have ended because of "trust issue," but smart women know what to do.

5. A relationship may no longer be a "love" relationship, but it can be a relationship.

6. There was a shift in my feelings for her.

7. You married a boy, then he became a man. He didn't change. He's the same but with gusto. Why are you mad now?

8. Men will always love cleavage and big butts. Ain't nothing changed. So get that operation for both body parts or buy those butt and breast pads.

9. You can be *not* so beautiful and have the big butt or the big breast and your stock just doubled.

10. Do you have the best part of him because you won't have all of him?

11. A man will rather live in a hoe house than his house.

12. There's so much friction as men get older. Everything changes, and they really don't know how to handle it.

13. They try to go back to their single days in their minds.

14. If they are married, the stress that they put on their wives is sometimes unbearable to the wife. The tiredness of having to go against this person wears her down.

15. She often hangs in there or she leaves because she had too! The husband never realizes or acknowledges this new behavior. The wife is now called crazy or jealous—go figure!

16. Men keep on until they are smitten. Sometimes they get caught. Sometimes they don't. It's in their DNA.

17. His ejaculation has nothing to do with you but everything to do with him.

18. By nature, men love sex, and women love men.

19. When you get married, you don't know who he or she is. After twenty-five years together, you really know who he or she is.

20. A woman can make a man do anything.

9 781984 570581